First published 2022 by Two Hoots. This edition published 2023 by Two Hoots an imprint of Pan Macmillan · The Smithson, 6 Briset Street, London, EC1M 5NR · EU representative: Macmillan Publishers Ireland Limited 1st Floor, The Liffey Trust Centre, 117-126 Sheriff Street Upper, Dublin 1, D01 YC43. Associated companies throughout the world. www.panmacmillan.com · ISBN 978-1-5098-5737-1 · Text and illustrations copyright © Emily Gravett 2022, 2023. Moral rights asserted. All rights reserved. No part of this publication may be reproduced, stored in a retrieval system, or transmitted, in any form or by any means (electronic, mechanical, photocopying, recording or otherwise), without the prior written permission of the publisher · 1 2 3 4 5 6 7 8 9 · A CIP catalogue record for this book is available from the British Library. Printed in China. The illustrations in this book were created using pencil and watercolour with a smidgen of digital fiddle faddling. www.twohootsbooks.com

This
TW🐾 HOOTS
book belongs to

. . . .

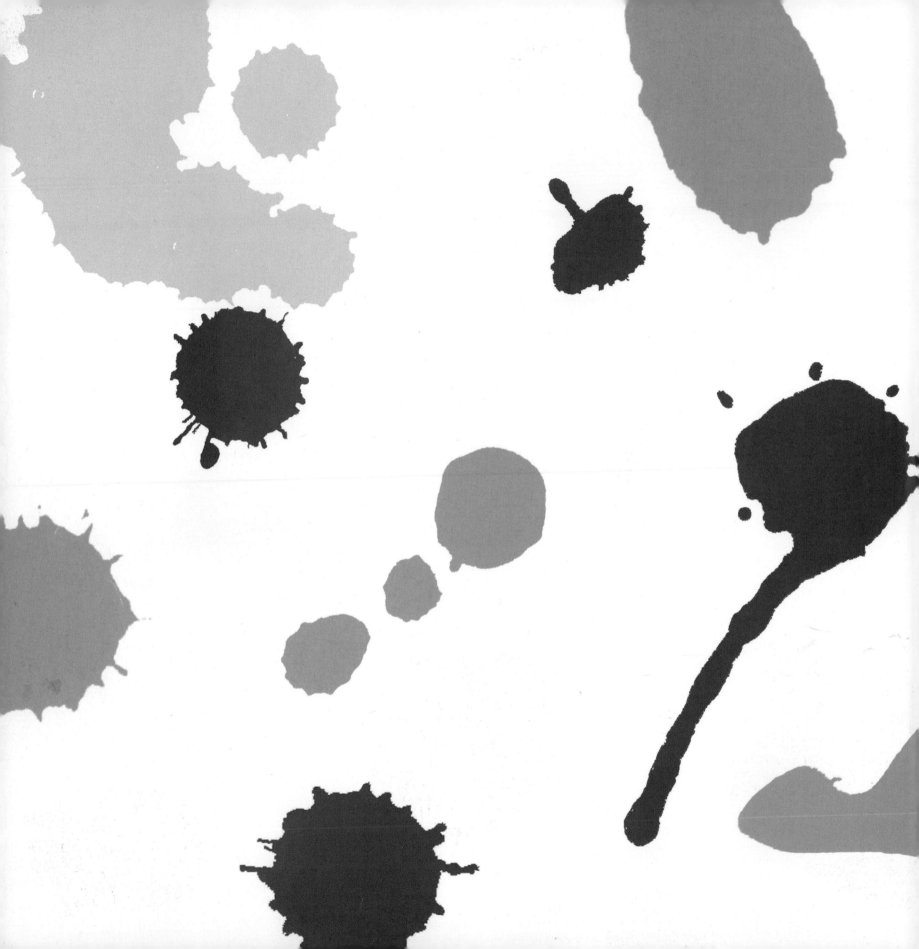

10 CATS

Emily Gravett

TWO HOOTS

10
cats

1
white cat

2
black cats

3
cats with stripes

4
cats with patches

5
cats with
red spots

6
cats with
yellow dots

7
cats with
blue blotches

8
cats with
orange splotches

9
cats with
green splats

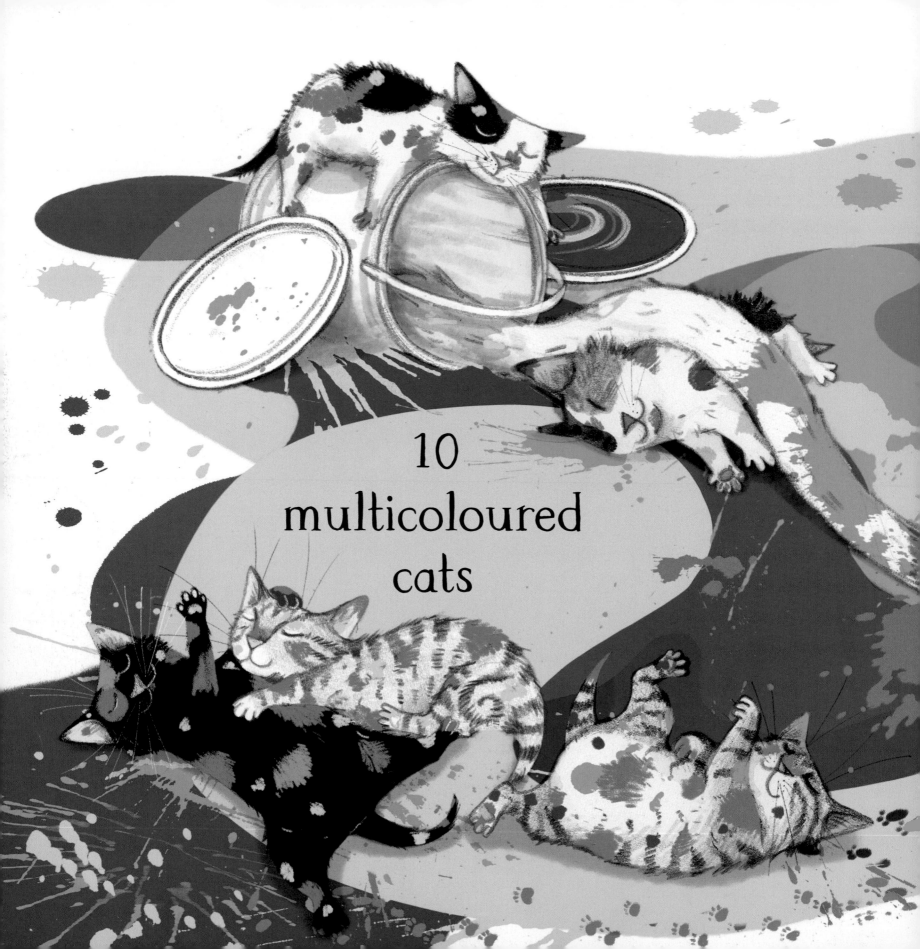

10
multicoloured
cats

Also from Emily Gravett

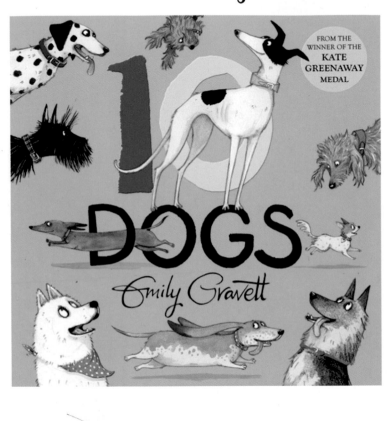

10 DOGS
Emily Gravett